First published in Great Britain in 2009 by
Frances Lincoln Children's Books
4 Torriano Mews,
Torriano Avenue, London NW5 2RZ
www.franceslincoln.com

This edition published 2009 by
Eerdmans Books for Young Readers
an imprint of Wm. B. Eerdmans Publishing Co.
2140 Oak Industrial Dr. NE
Grand Rapids, Michigan 49505
P.O. Box 163, Cambridge CB3 9PU U. K.

www.eerdmans.com/youngreaders

Printed in Singapore

15 14 13 12 11 10 09   9 8 7 6 5 4 3 2 1

Library of Congress Cataloging-in-Publication Data

Koralek, Jenny.
The story of Queen Esther / by Jenny Koralek ; illustrated by Grizelda Holderness.
p. cm.

ISBN 978-0-8028-5348-6 (alk. paper)

1. Esther, Queen of Persia—Juvenile literature. 1. Holderness, Grizelda, 1953- II. Title.
BS580.E8K67 2008
222'.909505—dc22
2008017713

Text type set in Angie
Illustrations created with pastels

The Story of Queen Esther

written by Jenny Koralek
illustrated by Grizelda Holderness

Eerdmans Books for Young Readers

Grand Rapids, Michigan • Cambridge, U.K.

There was once a rich and powerful king
who ruled over the land of Persia. Ahasuerus was
his name. He was a fierce soldier, but he also
loved to hold great feasts and to walk in his
beautiful gardens, which were famous
throughout the whole world.

One day the king decided he must have a wife. He sent for all the young girls in his vast kingdom and chose the most beautiful one. Her name was Esther.

Esther was an orphan who had been living with her cousin, Mordecai. He loved Esther as if she was his own daughter. Mordecai served the king faithfully. But he was not happy when the king chose Esther to be his wife.

"Promise me that you won't tell anyone that you are a Jew," he said as he kissed her goodbye. "Many people at the palace hate Jews because we were once their enemies."

"I promise," said Esther, and away she went to get ready for her wedding. Her seven maids bathed her in precious, sweet-smelling oils and brushed her hair until it shone.

When Esther appeared before the king dressed as a
bride, he crowned her with a golden crown. He ordered
a holiday for everyone and gave gold coins to all the
poor people in the city. Then he and Esther sat down
with hundreds of guests to a grand wedding feast.

That night, Mordecai overheard two royal guards plotting to kill the king. He quickly sent a message to Esther, who told the king, and the two men were arrested.

Mordecai had saved the king's life! His name was written down in the king's Book of Records — but the king soon forgot all about it.

Now, the king's most powerful advisor was his Grand Vizier, Haman. Everyone had to bow low whenever Haman appeared. But Mordecai never bowed down to him.

"Why don't you bow down to me?" Haman asked Mordecai one day.

"I am a Jew," said Mordecai, "and Jews bow down only to God."

Haman grew angrier and angrier with Mordecai. He decided to get rid of him — and all the Jews living in Persia. He sat down and drew lots with his friends to find the best day for killing the Jews. Then he went to the king and said, "Your Majesty, the Jews do not obey some of your laws. Why don't you get rid of them?"

The king gave his royal ring of command to Haman and said, "Do what you like with them."

When Mordecai heard the
terrible news, he quickly sent a
message to Esther: "Only you can
save us now! Go to the king and
beg him to be merciful."

Esther sent a message back:
"Anyone who goes before the king
uninvited will be put to death —
even I, the queen."

"You must go," Mordecai replied.

"Very well," said Esther, "I will go
to him. But first, you and I must fast
and pray to prepare ourselves."

For three days and three nights
Esther and Mordecai ate and
drank nothing.
Mordecai prayed for help.
Esther prayed for courage.

She was very frightened, but finally Esther went to the king, who was sitting on his great golden throne.

When he saw her coming before him uninvited, his face blazed with anger — and Esther fainted.

Then the king remembered how much he loved her. He leapt to his feet and took her in his arms.

"Esther! Esther!" he cried. "What is the matter? It must be something very important, for you to come to me uninvited."

"O great king!" said Esther, "I have just one favor to ask. Please be my guest tomorrow at a special dinner, and bring Haman with you."

The king agreed.

Haman was delighted and rushed home to tell his wife.

"Guess what? I have been invited to dine with the king and queen! That will show everyone just how important I am. Oh, happy day! The only thing spoiling it is that wretched Mordecai who refuses to bow down to me. What can I do about him?"

"Have a gallows built," said his wife, "and ask the king to have Mordecai hanged."

Haman thought that was a good idea and had a gallows built right away.

That night the king could not sleep a wink. So he sent for his Book of Records and had it read to him. When he heard how Mordecai had once saved his life, he asked, "And what was his reward?"

"There was no reward, Your Majesty," came the answer.

Early the next morning Haman came in, hoping to get the king's permission to hang Mordecai.

"Ah, Haman!" cried the king. "Tell me, how can I reward a man who has served me well?"

"Hmm," thought Haman, "he must be talking about me."

"Your Majesty," he replied, "dress him in royal robes, put him on the king's favorite horse, and lead him through the city among the cheering crowds."

"What a good idea!" cried the king. "Go and find Mordecai. See that he is dressed in splendid clothes and mounted on a fine horse, and you yourself shall lead him through the streets! And be sure to call out as you go, 'This good man saved the king's life.'"

Haman had to obey, but deep down he felt bitter and ashamed.

That evening after dinner, the king said to Esther, "And now, my queen, what can I do to please you? I love you so much, I would give you half my kingdom."

Esther took a deep breath. "No, Your Majesty," she replied, "that is not what I want." She paused.

"Go on," said the king. "You know I would give you anything."

"Your Majesty," Esther replied, "I want something far more precious. I want the lives of my people. You see, I am a Jew, and we are all going to be killed!"

"By whose order?" asked the king angrily. "Who would do such a terrible thing?"

"The man sitting beside you, Your Majesty," said Esther. "Haman."

The king was horrified. "Take him away and execute him!" he commanded.

And so Haman was hanged on the very same gallows he had built for Mordecai.

Then the king sent for Mordecai. "You shall be my new Grand Vizier," he said.

The first thing Mordecai did was tear up Haman's order to kill the Jews.

From that day on, Jews were treated like everyone else in Persia.

The Jews danced and sang with joy.

And to this day a noisy, happy feast, the Feast of Purim, is held every year to remember how Queen Esther saved the lives of her people.